MW00882156

Book Cover Illustration by John Berryman (DALL-E 3), edited by
Meg Berryman (Adobe Fresco)

1st edition 2024

The Wolf Pack

The Pride of the Alpha

by Meg Berryman

Chapter 1

"Come on, Delta!" Yelled Alpha.

"I'm coming! Wait! It takes a lot of strength to hold seven deer at once!" Delta responded. The wolves were coming back to their den, when all of a sudden they heard a gunshot.

"Wolf hunters." Alpha growled under her breath. "Everybody get inside. We're going to let Beta take care of this one."

Beta squealed, "Did someone say my name?!" As she rushed out the door, screamed at the sight of wolf hunters, and hid behind a huge boulder, Alpha walked over to the boulder and pushed it away with just a paw.

"Beta, you have to learn to not be scared of wolf hunters! I mean, yes they are annoying, but they're harmless!"

Beta whimpered,"But then why are they called wolf hunters?"

"Ugh. Beta, you are the daughter of the Alpha, and you shall become a great Alpha yourself!! So I, the Alpha, commands you to get rid of the wolf hunters!!" she yelled in her most commanding voice.

"O-ok, mom." Stuttered Beta. Beta climbed down the mountain, shivering in fear. She stumbled through the woods, tripping over small twigs and rocks. Then, Beta peeked her snout into a clearing and saw two wolf hunters with a wolf in their net.

"This will make a good fur coat for my wife." grunted the wolf hunter in the camo suit. Beta covered her mouth with a paw to keep herself from screaming. "What do I do? If I go into the clearing right now, I will most definitely get sho-oh wait! I have body armor! But they can capture me..." She whispered to herself.

While she thought about what to do, the other wolf hunter said,"I smell another wolf."

The first hunter said, "Jake, we already have a wolf here. I don't think we need another one. "

"Hey, don't you go on talking about that, Weston! My sense of smell never lies, and I want a fur coat myself." Jake snapped back.

"Alright, we'll take a look at it." Weston grumbled.

Chapter 2

Beta gasped as the wolf hunters sneaked toward her. She quietly ran along the edge of the clearing and hid behind a log. "What do I do?! I'm stuck in this clearing with two wolf hunters, and another wolf! Without my mom..." She whispered to herself.

"Please help me, I'm the one stuck in this net with wolf hunters that want to skin me!" Whimpered the other wolf.

"No, no, no, no, no! Be quiet or you'll get us both caught!" Shushed Beta.

But it was too late. Weston turned around and aimed his gun. Beta sliced through the net with her sharp claws and pulled the wolf out of the clearing. As soon as they were out of the danger, Beta grabbed the wolf and said, "I am the Beta of the Ultima Pack. Who are you, where do you live, and what are you doing in my territory?"

"W-wow! Are you really a Beta? Of the Ultima Pack?!" Iota bowed low. "Uh, my name is Iota, I live in Squirrel Forest, and I got lost and can't find my way back."

"Well Iota, since you are in MY territory, which is a mile in every direction from Great Wolf Mountain, I command you to be part of The Ultima Wolf Pack!" A bright light blinded everything in range.

Meanwhile, Alpha was strutting down the mountain, looking for a rabbit or two to snack on, when she thought about her daughter. "Hmm, I hope she comes back soon. Auuggh!" She yelled as a light as bright as the sun appeared in her vision. As the light faded, she took her paws off her eyes and said to herself, "A new wolf?"

As Beta finished the ritual, she heard a howl in the distance. "BETA!! I TOLD YOU NOT TO DO THE SACRED RITUAL WITHOUT MY PERMISSION!!"

Beta breathed in sharply and said timidly,"Oh, no I forgot! Well, come on Iota, it's time to meet your new Alpha."

Chapter 3

When Beta walked up the mountain, Gamma, one of her cousins, ran down to her. "Beta! Alpha's really upset at what you did. Come with me, I know a good hiding-"

"BETA!" Alpha cut off Gamma. She walked over to the two then said in a sarcastically sweet voice, "Now who is this little 'friend' you've got here?"

Beta blushed and said, "Umm, well... His name is Iota, and he's from Squirrel Forest. I think that's it."

Alpha said in a motherly voice, "Hm. Well, show him inside, and I'll get his room ready."

She turned to Gamma and said, "Now Gamma, I heard you talking to Beta about hiding from me. We're going to my room to have a little talk, alright?"

Gamma gulped. She knew what Alpha meant by "little talk".

They all walked inside when Beta whispered to Alpha, "Um, mom? I forgot to um, you know, the wolf hunters?"

Alpha stared at Beta until she got uncomfortable. "Hey mom???" Beta asked. Alpha said exasperatedly, "Ugh, you are sooo scared of humans. It's alright, I'll take care of them."

Then Alpha said noticeably louder, "And meanwhile, Epsilon will help Beta with her hunting lessons!"

Epsilon yelled back very annoyed, "SERIOUSLY?!"

Alpha shook her head in irritation. "Epsilon, I know how you are with Beta, but give her a chance! She's going to be an Alpha, so I need you to teach her to act like one!"

Epsilon grumbled, "Oh, fine."

Beta giggled, "Mom, aren't you going to have a little talk with Gamma?"

Gamma looked at Beta and shook her head furiously.

Alpha grinned and said, "Oh yes! I forgot! Well you don't forget about showing Iota around! Remember, you did the Sacred Ritual without me, so I'm taking away your free time."

After Alpha left, she turned to Iota and said, "After I'm done showing you the den, I'm going to show you a secret!"

Iota shrugged and said, "Well, I'm fine with that if I'm welcome here!"

Beta showed Iota the dining room, the first to the left of the hallway. He was amazed at how big and polished the room was! And the seats were covered with soft, cushy, deer fur.

Then she showed him the meeting room, and then she touched a certain area of the rock with her paw, and it turned out to be a trapdoor!

Inside was a small cave where she wove a beautiful tapestry of her family/pack.

When she showed Iota this, she said, "Now that you're part of the pack, I'm going to have to weave you on this thing."

He replied, "I think it looks beautiful without me."

Beta blushed at this comment and said shyly, "Thanks."

When they got out of the meeting room, she showed Iota the entrance to Alpha's room, and said, "No one goes in here without Alpha's permission. I don't need to show you the other rooms, so I'll show you my secret now."

Chapter 4

"Come on! Don't be lazy." Said Beta as she ran and wove through the winding branches of Great Wolf Forest.

"I'm coming. Wait! You're so fast!" Said Iota, stumbling and climbing over the branches. "*This forest is unlike the one I used to live in. It's so beautiful!*" Thought Iota.

Beta smiled and said, "You know I can read your mind. Thanks!"

Iota's snout turned red in embarrassment.
"Oh."

Beta suddenly looked up and sniffed the air.
She gasped and said, "We're near Maydrop.
Did I go the wrong way?"

Iota looked at her curiously. "Um, may I
ask... What's Maydrop?"

Beta said, "A human town. I think I went the
wrong way. No offense, but I think you
distracted me. Come on, I know the direction
our destination is from here. It'll just take a
little bit longer."

Finally, after 20 minutes, they arrived. Iota's
jaw dropped when he saw the clearing where
there were trees spotted randomly.

Beta laughed in enthusiasm as she jumped from tree to tree. "Come on, lazybones! It's a parkour arena!"

Iota stuttered, "W-what? How did you make this?"

Beta laughed again and said, "I found it! Now come up here and play!"

As the two played and laughed together, Iota felt something he had never felt before. He felt from that point… he had a crush on her.

As they walked up Great Wolf Mountain, Beta saw Alpha running down to her with a worried look on her face. "Where have you two been? I was worried sick!" Alpha hugged her daughter.

Beta looked at her mother in embarrassment and disgust. "Mom! Not in front of another wolf!"

Alpha kissed her daughter on the tip of her snout and said, "Well, young lady, what do you have to say for yourself?"

Beta eyed her mom and said, "Ok, ok, I will come home earlier."

"And?"

"Ugh, I won't go out without your permission."

"Aand?"

"Mom! Stop pushing it! Argh, I love you."

"Alright, Beta. DON'T do it again. I'm watching you."

Alpha turned to Iota and said, "And you, why did you let her run off like that? I want her to grow up responsible. You let her run off and be childish! Well, come inside both of you. Epsilon's lucky he didn't have to give you hunting lessons."

Alpha sniffed and turned around. When she strolled into the dining room with Beta and Iota, she immediately saw Gamma halfway through a bite of deer rib. "GAMMA! I SAID NO DINNER!" Alpha yelled in anger.

Gamma said with her mouth full, "Bu I humbry!"

"I DON'T CARE IF YOU'RE HUNGRY! I SAID NO DINNER AND THAT'S FINAL!" Alpha yelled.

Gamma glared at Beta.

Iota whispered to Beta, "Boy, is the Alpha strict."

Beta nodded in agreement.

Alpha said, "I heard that."

Iota's snout turned red again.

Alpha called for Epsilon and said, "Well, we're not going to stand here and stare at each other are we? Who wants dinner?!"

Gamma grumbled, "I do."

The wolves went into the dining room and started to eat.

Chapter 5

Beta and Iota walked out of the dining room full and satisfied. Iota said, "Wow, that was the best food I've had in a while!"

Beta winked and whispered, "My mom's specialty is cooking."

Alpha turned to the two and said to Iota, "Iota, I will lead you to your room from here. Beta, It's time for bed."

Beta said exasperatedly, "Mom! I'm not a pup anymore! I can go to bed myself."

Beta went into her geode bedroom and fell into a wonderful sleep.

Early the next morning, Alpha gently nudged her sleeping daughter awake. "Wake up, my little pup! It's time to go hunting."

Alpha left the room. Right after she left, Beta peeked one eye open, sat up, and yawned. "*That was a good sleep. I'm gonna go see if Iota is already awake.*" She thought to herself.

Beta tottered off to Iota's room, and when she opened the door, a gorgeous red light reflected off the crimson rubies.

Iota woke up instantly when he heard small paws pattering on the floor beside him. "Oh! Uh, hi Great Beta."

Beta looked at him annoyed and said, "You can be a little more casual than that. Come on, it's hunting time! My personal favorite."

The pack ran outside and Alpha ordered there to be two groups that would split up. "Group number one! Beta, Epsilon, and Iota! You go behind the mountain. It's rich with elk and deer. Beta, I think your friend Alice lives at the base of Great Wolf Mountain, in the direction you're heading. Alright, group number two! Me, Delta, and Gamma! We're going to head into Maydrop to see if we can sneak pizza. I know it's famous for pizza and you all know I love pizza. Now split!" Alpha barked.

Alpha, Delta, and Gamma navigated the forest until they got to Maydrop. "Alright team, we're heading in from the main entrance."

Delta whispered nervously, "I must have heard you wrong. The MAIN entrance?!"

Alpha smiled mischievously. "No, no, you heard me right. I said the main entrance. YOU forgot that we had human disguises." Alpha then howled in the key of C and instantly transformed into a human.

To show the other wolves that she was the Alpha in human form, she had light blue streaks through her hair, she had a scar on the back of her hand, and she had electric blue eyes. Her clothing was much more casual than someone would expect an Alpha in human form would wear. She had a light gray hoodie on that was open in the middle, and her shirt was navy blue with a picture of a wolf on it. The caption was "Runnin' with the

Wolves!" The hood was pulled over her head. She wore leggings that were white and matched her white sneakers. She had black socks pulled to her ankles.

Gamma and Delta howled in the key of C and they both transformed into what looked close to Alpha in human form, just without the scar and they each had their own theme colors.

"Alright, everybody get in. Let's go grab some pizza." Said Alpha.

Chapter 6

"Alpha, I don't like this..." Whined Delta as they walked through the huge crowd in the market.

"I don't either, Delta. Something's suspicious. Why are there so many people? Wait. Stop." Alpha said. She sniffed the air and growled under her breath. "No... It can't be. Magnus."

At the front of the crowd was a big stage where they elected the mayor. On that stage there were two contestants. Someone they didn't know, and Magnus, their nemesis.

Someone from the crowd squealed, "Ooh, he's so handsome!"

Alpha laughed roughly and said, "Handsome? Oh yeah right. That girl better see all his scars from his past battles with me."

Gamma leaned over to Alpha and said, "Alpha, I just went to see the voting booth, and he's going to be mayor by a landslide of votes!"

Alpha looked toward the voting booth and said, "Hm. Not on my watch."

Meanwhile, Beta was walking over to Alice's cave at the base of Great Wolf Mountain.

"Alice? Aaalice! I'm hunting! do you want to join me?" Beta said playfully.

No response.

"*Hm, she's probably sleeping. I'll go in and wake her up. She's soo lazy.*" Beta thought. Beta screamed when a pair of black wolves jumped out from the cave and grabbed her. "Epsilon! Help me! Iota! Mrph!"

They covered her mouth so she couldn't yell for help. Then the shadow wolves dragged her into the cave and tied her up.

Beta looked around and saw Alice on the floor with cuts and bruises.

"I-I'm sorry Beta. They threatened to kill me!" Alice whispered feebly.

Beta sighed. "It's not your fault. I should have listened to Epsilon when he told me to wait for him. Now look what I've gotten us into!" Beta said sadly.

"Hey. Enough of the talk. Come with us." The black wolves grabbed Beta and Alice and they threw Alice into a side cave. She hit her head on a rock and passed out. The kidnappers rolled a boulder over the mouth of the cave.

"No! Alice! Hey, that's animal cruelty!" Beta screamed when they threw her best friend into the cave.

"Hey, we don't care. You're the one we want." Growled one of the wolves.

They grabbed her and tied her paws together. Then they held her roughly by the arms and gagged her. "We're taking you to our cave on

Starfish Bay. You'll never escape us until your so-called 'Alpha' gives up all of her land." They laughed when they thought about the look on the Alpha's face when she realized that her daughter was missing.

When they reached their cave, the wolves dragged her deeper into the damp and dark cave.They threw her into a small cell in the deepest, darkest part of the cave. Beta scrambled to her feet the moment she hit the ground and tried to squeeze through the door before they shut it. She was too late.

She sat down in her cell and cried. "Why did I have to be kidnapped by the Shadow Wolf Pack? I want to be with my mom and Iota!" She sobbed.

Beta overheard the other wolves talking about their own personal business. "When is show-off Magnus coming back? It's been a while."

"That's because you didn't capture her fast enough!"

"No, it was easy to capture her. As easy as it is to lure you into a dragon's mouth with a slab of deer meat!"

The wolves all started laughing except the one who was insulted.

Beta stared at the floor. The only comfort to her was the light that her body was emitting. "*Wait, I'm glowing?*" thought Beta.

Chapter 7

"Oh, Beta where did you go? This isn't funny anymore!" Yelled Epsilon as he and Iota searched for Beta. "*Where is she? Alpha's going to be so mad at me...*" Epsilon thought.

"Beta!! Beeeta!!" Yelled Iota. "*I hope she's okay. I would feel terrible if something happened to her. I really like her!*" Thought Iota.

Epsilon said, "I feel the same. Even if she is the MOST ANNOYING WOLF IN THE WORLD, I would hate it if something happened to her. She is my little niece."

Iota looked away because his face turned red again. "*How do they read my mind?*"

"Wait! I've got a scent. Oh no. You are kidding me." Shushed Epsilon.

"What?" Asked Iota curiously.

"Shadow wolves. Stupid evil creatures that practice black magic. I'm pawing the spot and then we're going to tell Alpha." Epsilon hit the ground with his paw and suddenly, a bright light shot up and glowed above the spot.

"But won't that just worry her?"

"Of course it will, but we need backup. Get your human disguise on, because we're going to Maydrop."

"Wait! Not yet, I hear something."

Epsilon and Iota walked over to Alice's cave. They rolled away the boulder and as soon as they walked inside, they saw Alice on the floor.

"Alice!" Epsilon quickly picked up the hurt wolf and brought her to the safety of their own cave.

"Will she be okay?" Iota asked.

"Yes, she will, but she needs rest. Now come on! Let's go to Maydrop!" Epsilon urged.

As soon as they walked in with their human disguises, someone grabbed them from behind and said in a low voice, "Are you the ones that messed up my mayorship? Speak up."

Epsilon said, "No, Magnus, I have no idea what you are talking about."

Then all of a sudden Epsilon kicked Magnus in the leg and they both ran as fast as they could. "Alpha! Come here!" Epsilon yelled.

Alpha and the rest of her group came running over. "What's wrong? And why isn't Beta with you?"

"That's the problem! Beta was kidnapped from right under my snout!"

Alpha screamed at the top of her lungs, "WHAT?! WHERE IS SHE?!"

Meanwhile, back in her prison, Beta looked at her glowing paws. "What is this magic?" She aimed a beam of light at the door of her cell. "Dang." She said grumpily when it didn't open.

Then she aimed it at the ground and out popped a bunch of glowing flowers. "Oh. Neat. I'm the wolf of gardening now." She said disappointedly. When she reached out to touch the flowers, a purple fire shot up.

"Wha-? Woah. Sweet." She aimed it at a different patch of ground and flowers sprang up there too.

"I hope these are different." She said quietly and hopefully. When she reached out to touch them, she was knocked back.

"Oof. Nice!" She said while rubbing her head. Then she thought, "*They're mine, so I must be able to control them. Please don't knock me back*." She thought.

She reached for the flowers and this time, she was able to touch them. "This is so cool! I have powers!" Beta said gleefully.

"I'm back! Where are you guys?" Said Magnus an hour later as he strutted into the cave. No one noticed the shadows following him.

Chapter 8

"Everybody get in. Quietly and not too quickly, we don't want to get in front of Magnus! Don't let Magnus or his goons find us." Whispered Alpha.

Iota thought about Beta and all the trouble she was in. "*I hope I'm the one to find her. Then maybe she'll like me. A lot.*"

Meanwhile, Beta sat in her cell and thought about what had happened in the past few days.

First, she had befriended Iota. Next, she showed him her tapestry and he actually liked it! After that, she had gone on a hunting trip that had turned out to be part of a kidnapping spree. Lastly, she had gotten powers.

It then came to her that a lot of it was with Iota. "Does he like me? Like, like me? Maybe..."

"I'm home, I said!" Beta rolled her eyes. Magnus always had to make a spectacular entrance.

Her eyes widened.

Magnus was HOME.

She shook the bars as hard as she could. They didn't budge. She was breathing quickly now, thinking hard. "*What do I do? What do I do? Ok, Stay calm, think this through. I'm calm now, and I'm stuck in a prison with my worst enemies being the ones that captured me. I have no ways out unless my mom or someone finds me. Oh, I hope Alice is okay.*"

Suddenly, something hit the bars. HARD.

Beta saw the red tinted outline of… "Iota? I can't see you, so you must be camouflaged!"

"Shush!"

"Wha- What are you doing here?"

"The rest of the pack is here too, but I just decided to go ahead."

"No, just tell the rest where I am! Th-"

Beta was cut off by Magnus noisily announcing that he would go see their prisoner. "Iota, run! Now!"

Iota finally turned around, but he was too late.

Magnus saw Beta sitting in her cell, but he felt that something was wrong. He saw a red glow in the corner, and so he walked over to it and poked the source.

"Ow!" was all that he needed to hear before he dragged Iota over to the cell by his neck, opened the door, kicked Beta away, and threw Iota in. "Beta, your 'mom' is going to have to give me her home to get you back, and all her prized land. HAHAHAHA!"

"Oh Magnus, you fool." Beta snapped at him.

Iota looked toward her dreamily. "*Wow, she's so cute when she's upset.*" He thought.

"Excuse me?" Asked Beta, frowning.

"Oh, nothing, nothing." "*Dang, I did it again.*"

"Iota, let's try to find a way out of here. Ooh! Ooh! I want to show you the powers that I got!"

"You got powers? Cool! So did I! The Alpha gave me them. Show me your powers first."

"Ok, watch this." Beta aimed a beam of light at the ground and out popped dark purple flowers that illuminated the cave.

"Whoa, cool."

"Wait, but that's not all! Try to touch them." Iota reached out for them, and he was knocked back. "Wow! Awesome!"

"I have another one, except it's fire. *Purple* fire."

"The Alpha gave me the power to control and make fire and lava! We can use my power to get us out of here!" Iota said enthusiastically.

"Oh yeah! You can melt through the bars and get us out!" Said Beta quietly. Twenty minutes later, Beta and Iota emerged from the cell.

"Wow, that was really burning hot. You singed my fur!"

"Sorry."

"You're alright, it's nothing to worry about."
Beta smiled at him.

Iota blushed. Beta's ears suddenly perked up.
"I hear a battle going on. Come on Iota, I
love battles!"

They went outside just in time to see Magnus
throw Alpha into the ocean.

"YOU'LL NEVER DEFEAT ME!
HAHAHAHA! I AM THE TRUE ALPHA!"

Alpha winced as she got back on her paws.
She looked toward Beta and said, "A true
Alpha... IS ONE THAT ALWAYS GETS
BACK UP!!"

Alpha yelled a victory yell and threw Magnus
with all her might into the depths of the
Unforgiving Ocean.

"Mom, is he gone?"

Alpha took a few breaths and then said, "No, dear, he'll find his way back up. Meanwhile, we should be helping Epsilon. He's being attacked by Thunder, the Shadow Wolf that's and-"

"Weston. One of the best wolf hunters in the country. One of the ones that captured Iota before I met him."

"Wow, I'm amazed that a human found his way here." Alpha said.

"Come on guys, Let's go fight!" Said Iota.

Chapter 9

Epsilon slashed at Thunder with his razor sharp claws.

Thunder laughed and said, "Ha ha ha! You might have beat our Alpha, but you can't beat me!"

Epsilon jumped to the side as a bullet flew under his arm. "You'll regret this, Thunder."

"Oh, I won't. I'll beat you!" Thunder laughed again as if he were merely enjoying it.

Epsilon hit him in the leg, which in turn knocked Thunder to his back. Epsilon jumped on top of Thunder and pinned him to the ground. Epsilon growled, about to finish him off, but he hesitated thinking, "*This is murder. Why would I murder a fellow wolf? The world is cruel.*"

Thunder noticed Epsilon's hesitation and took the chance. He flipped himself to his feet, then while Epsilon was still off balance, grabbed him so Epsilon was in a disadvantaged position. "HAHAHAHAHA! Fortune favors the powerful!" He struck Epsilon with his claws then threw him to the ground as if he was a rag doll.

Beta screamed and ran over to her uncle. "Epsilon! Talk to me. Please!" She sobbed. "No!"

Beta picked him up and carried him to a spot where he couldn't be found. She laid down next to him and cried.

A glimmer of light fell from her eyes to the forest floor and soaked into the ground. A flower sprang up and glowed with a hopeful light. Slowly, the wound on Epsilon's chest healed. Epsilon opened his eyes and sat up. "Beta? Why are you crying?"

Beta gasped and looked up when she heard Epsilon's voice. Epsilon wiped a tear from her eye.

"I thought you died!" Stuttered Beta.

Epsilon smiled and said, "I still need to recover though. Go get some revenge! And here's a tip: Never hesitate. Now go, Beta!" After he said this, he flopped down and tried to sleep.

Beta ran to the battlefield where Thunder was now taking on Gamma and Delta, laughing like a madman. Beta shrieked when Thunder almost sliced off Delta's arm. Beta ran faster than Alpha had ever ran and bit Thunder on the shoulder.

Thunder screamed in pain and ran into the forest, never to be seen again. "What a wimp." Beta remarked.

Gamma and Delta gaped in awe at the wolf that beat the monster that they thought was unbeatable. "Wow. Just wow. I forgive you for telling on me and making me lose my dinner." Said Gamma.

Beta smirked and said, "Well, this is not the time to stand around! We have to go help Alpha-"

SPLAT! Lightning the wolf, known for headbutting, ran into Beta after being chased away by Iota. Beta nodded in approval.

A few minutes later, Alpha walked over with a gun in her mouth. She spit it out and said, "Well, that was easy. Weston's also a wimp."

Epsilon came stumbling out from the hiding place that Beta had hid him in. "I think I can fight now. I'm just a little more cautious."

Iota walked over from his second battle with Lightning. "That one took a little more brain. Apparently, headbutting a tree does not work. All I had to do was stand in front of a tree and side-step him." He pointed toward the wolf on the ground, knocked out from running head first into a tree.

"COME AT ME!"

Every wolf turned around to see Knucklehead, the Beta of the Black Wolf Pack. "HA! ALL THE OTHERS ARE WIMPS! TRY ME! I BET YOU'RE WIMPS TOO!"

Alpha turned to the other pack members. "Let's do this."

An hour into the battle, Iota thought, "This is it. Now or never." He turned to Beta. She looked like she was enjoying this. He didn't want to ruin the moment for her, but as he thought, it was now or never.

He grabbed Beta and pulled her out of the battle to the edge of the beach. *He would tell her.*

Chapter 10

"Iota, let me go! What are you doing?!" Beta looked at Iota surprised.

"Beta, there's something I have to tell you." Beta squinted at Iota, trying to read his mind. She took a step back when she couldn't do it. She always could do it! But there was something more powerful than her powers. What was this powerful magic? "What do you have to tell me?" She said softly.

"I-I lov- Argh! I can't do it."

"Get over your fears. I'm ready to hear whatever you have to tell me." She said kindly. Tears fell from Iota's eyes. She was so beautiful. "I love you."

Beta gasped. "Y-you're not kidding?!"

Iota looked at her sincerely. "No. I love you."

Beta, still surprised, took Iota's paws. She whispered, "I love you too. I've secretly loved you since the time we met."

There in the moonlight, in the midst of the battle, the wolves kissed. Then they turned to the fight. Beta looked at Iota and nodded. "Let's do this." They charged, with new confidence towards the battle.

Alpha saw them and said, "Take the left legs! We need him off balance!"

Iota, with newfound strength slashed at Knucklehead's paws. Beta, at the same time, grew blood-red flowers around his legs. The damage from the fire flowers and the dagger-like claws knocked the evil wolf to his back. "AAGH! HELP ME!"

Alpha looked at the giant wolf rolling around on his back like a ball and said, "He's so big he can't get over on his feet! He's like a giant turtle! Everybody, please don't look. I'm going to turn into my Ultimate form and banish him to the ends of the Unforgiving Ocean."

Beta whispered to Iota, "If a human looks at an Alpha in human form, they just won't exist anymore. One look and poof! They're gone.

Of course, we're fine." "Oh, and it's supposed to look terrifying." She added.

Every wolf heard Knucklehead's scream when Alpha turned into her Ultimate form.

Beta winced and continued, "The lower the rank of wolf they are, the less horrific the sight would be. Alpha is the highest ranked wolf in the highest ranked pack."

"I'm finished! You can turn around now."

Every wolf let out a breath of relief. They all turned around at the same time and Knucklehead was gone.

Suddenly, Magnus came sputtering and spitting out saltwater out of the Unforgiving Ocean. "I'll-huff-get you!"

Alpha grabbed him by his neck and said, "Magnus YOU MONSTER! KIDNAPPING MY DAUGHTER AND HOLDING HER HOSTAGE! WHY I OUGHTA-"

Beta shook her head. "*Moms. Always protective.*" She smiled. "Mom, can I have him?"

Alpha threw Magnus like a Frisbee to Beta. Beta whispered in his ear, "I pity you. I really do. I don't know what made you so evil, but you should know that everybody here is sad for you."

"I'm sorry!" Magnus whimpered.

Beta responded, "I wish I was sorry too." Then she tossed him in his cave.

Finally at home, Beta went to Iota's room and just stayed with him.

A few minutes later, Epsilon went into Iota's room and was going to tell him to come to dinner, but stopped at the sight of his niece and Iota kissing. "Iota! time to come to- What in the world? Why are you kissing Beta?" Epsilon gaped at the pair.

Iota blushed and turned away. Beta looked annoyingly at Epsilon.

Epsilon snickered and said, "Well, you two lovebirds have to come to dinner. I can't stand without dinner for long! Race you there, Beta!"

Beta stood up and ran to the dining room. "I win!" She looked at Epsilon and smirked.

Epsilon smiled back at her. "Hey, thanks for bringing me back to life."

"You're welcome, zombie brain."

"HEY!!"

Beta laughed and skipped over to her seat. "Alice, come here! You should feel fine now, right?"

"I'm coming!"

Iota sat down next to Beta and they shared a smile. Beta looked at the giant plate in the middle. It had a giant-

"PIZZA!" everybody gasped.

"How did you do it, mom?" Beta asked curiously.

Alpha winked. "No matter what the situation, I can always grab a pizza."

Everybody laughed.

The Gem of Alphas shone brighter than ever that night.

May the Ultima's howl never die out! AWOOOOOOOO!

The Wolf Pack: Epilogue

Beta sat in the meeting room, discussing new ways to hunt and where the Shadow Wolves have moved their home. She had a big responsibility, being the new Alpha of the pack. She had figured that her mother needed a break.

After the meeting, Beta called on Iota to help her get to the parkour arena that they had known since they were 15.

She became Alpha at an early age. The natural year for crowning was at 25, but she was crowned at 22.

"Is he getting frisky?" Iota said.

Beta smiled. "Yep. He's very energetic today." She patted her belly. "He's going to be my little Beta. As I once was. Oof." Beta stumbled as she got up. "Before we go, can I go see Ultra-Alpha?"

"Sure."

Ultra-Alpha is what they called a retired Alpha. Kind of like retiring from a job. Beta winced as the pup inside of her kicked and struggled to get into the world.

"He wants to get out doesn't he?"

"Sure does! Oh, here comes my mother." Alpha strutted out from the room that had once been Beta's. "Oh! Beta! How is the little one?"

"Very energetic, Ultra-Alpha."

"Just call me mom, young lady. When you say that, it makes me feel old. Oh, you're growing so fast!" Alpha gave Beta a quick peck on the cheek. "Go have some fun. I'll stay here and manage the pack. DELTA! THAT WAS YOUR THIRTY-THIRD SNACK! GET OUT OF THE DINING ROOM! Epsilon, can you get me a bowl of water? I'm very thirsty right now."

Beta laughed as a grumpy Delta came out of the dining room. "Delta! You greedy wolf! It's like your stomach is always empty."

Iota put his paw on her shoulder. "We better get going. Beta's muscles don't like to rest for long!" The wolves laughed happily.

Magnus sat on his bed/mat in the middle of his new room, staring at a photo of a pup having a birthday party with his friends and parents. Tears of envy and sadness filled Magnus's eyes as he threw the picture to the ground. He didn't have real friends. His family hated him. Everyone thought he was worthless. He thought the other wolves didn't know how powerful he was. But he was the one that didn't know; he didn't know how much the wolves really were sad for him.

He put his face in his paws and cried. "I want a family that loves me! I hate it, I hate it, I hate it, how peaceful and happy the Ultimas and other wolves are!"

He remembered when his parents broke up, the hate pulling them apart. He remembered how his own mother, who he had been left with, threw him away to a wolf orphanage. How no one wanted him. How he had decided to show the world all the pain, the agony that it had shown him, and even now, it did him no good. "*Why is this not working? Why does everybody hate me so much? Why am I doomed to this fate?*" He thought. Just even saying it hurts.

He flopped down and fell asleep.

Made in the USA
Columbia, SC
17 November 2024

46437903R00040